Libby and the Cape of Visitability

By Eleanor Smith & Nadeen Green

Tuesday, July 10th.

I know that I shouldn't complain about my friends Aria and Benjamin. Well, I could, and sometimes I really want to, but I know that I shouldn't. After all, they are good friends and even when we do have fights, they are just quibbles. I love the word "quibble" – in fact, I like (adore, relish, delight in, savor) lots of words that sometimes my friends don't even know. I don't mean to sound all braggy and super smart here, but words are truly my thing. And I am always helping my friends with their vocabulary and spelling tests. Sometimes they call me Lib-Bee the Spelling Bee. But since I need to be honest here (because that is what this journal is supposed to be all about, sharing my thoughts and feelings because this is the summer assignment for school – how crummy that we have a summer assignment, I mean, is that really the right thing to do to us?), I guess I should mention that while I am super-good (a maestro, in fact) with words, math is not my friend. I haven't figured out when in my grownup life I will ever need long division or square roots or an x-axis and a y-axis or any algebra at all (maybe fractions, but I am not totally convinced about that either). So I really do appreciate when Aria and Benjamin help me with my math homework.

And they have even come to my rescue. Kids like me get teased a lot, and I can usually handle that (I once heard my Dad tell my Mom that I got my self-esteem from his side of the family; Mom didn't seem to exactly agree with that). But sometimes the teasing can be scary. Like when the three skuzzy boys who are a grade ahead of me in school decided to see if they could make me dizzy. We had just finished with PE class and these smelly sweaty slime balls (I am good with words for sure – that is great alliteration) surrounded me and spun me around and around and everything was out of control. I thought I was going to be flung halfway across the gym.

It was pretty awful when some of the other kids saw what was happening and started to cheer for my tormentors. I was terrified and worried that I would wet my pants and how would I ever cope with that; it wasn't my life that flashed before my eyes, it was my future. I saw myself being homeschooled because I wasn't ever coming back to school if that happened. But then Benjamin started yelling - at everybody! And when Aria ran over and actually kicked one of the goons in the legs, some of the other kids started to cheer for her and that turned the tide in my favor. Aria likes to remind me a lot about how she saved the day, but I have always thought that the basketball coach running into the gym (and yelling like everyone else only way louder) had something to do with that. But still, it was pretty brave of her to do what she did – and Benjamin, too.

Wednesday, July 11th.

Mom and Dad are always talking about how wonderful it is that me and Aria and Benjamin have been friends forever. And when they say forever, they mean it. Our families all lived here in this apartment building when we were born. Sometimes I like to look through our family photos and sort of watch us all grow up right before my eyes. There is my baby self with baby Aria and baby Benjamin (I have a definite opinion on who was the cutest baby, but even with the "journal honesty" thing, I am not about to share that opinion). There are some embarrassing pictures of all three of us in a bath tub together (at least all of our parts are covered by bubbles; I cannot imagine what on earth my parents were thinking when they took *that* photo).

There is a picture of us on our one year "group" birthday smearing frosting all over ourselves and each other, too. We were all born in May – but we have different zodiac signs because Aria and Benjamin were born early in the month and I was born later on May 28th. That makes me a Gemini – and that means that I am "confident, strong, independent and freedom-loving". I realize that I can't be as independent as lots of other people, but I am very confident (except when it comes to that bullying stuff). Our parents would put us in the bucket swings at the playground together and one time Benjamin threw up when the grownups were pushing us— puke went everywhere (which was very vomitous). Thankfully no one got a picture of that, but the photo of us in the swings is kind of cute – thankfully it was taken before Benjamin's explosive spewing (yuck). On our first day of kindergarten I was sitting between Aria and Benjamin in my push chair for the "First Day of School Photo". I see that picture all the time - it has been on the refrigerator door here in our apartment for years.

Friday, July 13th.

I know I am writing a lot about Aria and Benjamin, But they are kind of why I decided to do this for my journal in the first place. When I write down some of the neat things we did together it helps me to remember more about our friendship. And that is important to me, because I am not sure just where our friendship is going these days (but I am not ready to write about that yet either). I think I will stop writing for now...

Monday, July 16th.

When I got my power wheelchair it was halfway through second grade. With my power chair, all I have to do is push on the joy stick and the motor kicks in. I can drive fast or slow, according to what speed I set on the control box that's attached to the chair arm. I thought I was pretty hot stuff for a seven year old and I liked the attention that the chair got me. Remember that I am a freedom loving Gemini and I could get around without waiting for someone to push me or carry me – after all, I wasn't a baby anymore. And I guess the power chair was a pretty big deal for Mom and Dad, too. After all, I was getting heavier all the time, and it can't be the easiest thing to carry your child or to have to push her every time she needs to go from one place to another.

And wow, was my chair a big hit with Aria and Benjamin. When we went to the park I was the engine for a roller skating chain. Even kids that we didn't know or usually didn't play with would join in and the grown ups called it Libby's Conga Line. (I didn't know what that meant, so I recently looked it up on my computer. I think that doing a roller skating chain is definitely much cooler than all of those old-time people doing a silly dance, not that I plan to tell my parents that).

So me having the power chair was a good thing for everyone. At the Children's Museum I could go from one exhibit to another by myself, whenever I was ready. At the library I didn't have to ask someone to push me over to another book shelf – off I went. Even now I appreciate what having my "wheels" means. Our parents can drop me, Aria and Benjamin at the movie theater and I can zip around getting my ticket, my candy, and my soda all by myself – and I even have a cup holder for my soda. Aria and Benjamin can sit in seats right next to me because there is special seating – I don't have to sit off by myself, which wouldn't make sense at all when you go to the movies with friends. Aria does come with me to the bathroom. I could get there myself of course and manage just fine, but girls always go to the restrooms together in public. It is, as Benjamin points out while making a face, "what girls do".

One time when Aria and I were in the bathroom before the movie started, an old lady was in there too. My mom would think I am being disrespectful by calling her old, but I think she was almost 100 years old – really! - she was positively hoary (I read that word in a magazine and Dad said it means super-old, like ancient). Anyway, I remember her not just because she had a power chair but because she started to lecture me. All I had done was complain to Aria that the paper towels were where I couldn't reach them and then this lady who I had never seen before in my whole life started to yell at me.

She said why was I going around griping about paper towels because when she was a kid you could not even get through the doors of the bathroom stalls. She said that I can get around in my chair today because of her generation of disabled people fighting and even going to jail to change things. She went on and on about how fortunate I am to be KWD today. She told me that she couldn't go to movies with her friends like I do, or ball games, or some of the stores and restaurants because even in her smaller push chair she couldn't fit through doors or go up stairs or over curbs. She told me how I better appreciate all the ramps and curb cuts and wide doors and bathroom grab bars because I don't know what it is like not to be able to go places because of obstacles.

It is a good thing that I have a great vocabulary since she was kind of ranting about how I was a "beneficiary" of "legislation" that "resulted from advocacy". There was one scary moment when I looked at Aria who was rolling her eyes. I thought they would get stuck in her eye sockets. I thought I was going to start to laugh out loud and not be able to stop. Aria was definitely bored by the entire conversation (it wasn't really a conversation, it was a lecture) and she made sure to tell Benjamin about the lady and how Aria thought we would never get out of the bathroom in time for the movie previews (which I sometimes like more than the movies we see).

I guess I was a little more interested than I thought (and certainly more interested than Aria) though, because I remember that the lady talked about "ADA". I've seen that on my toothpaste tube (yes, ladies and gentlemen, I brush my teeth with paste that is approved by the ADA, aren't you glad to know that!) but that wasn't the ADA she meant. When I looked it up on my computer, I figured out it wasn't the dental association, it was D for Disabilities. Way back in 1990 they made a law that all public places have to be built in a way that lets people with disabilities get to them and in them and move around and pretty well do what people who don't have disabilities get to do. It's called The Americans with Disabilities Act. I guess it is true that I am lucky I was born when I was.

By the way, someone reading this might be wondering why I use a wheelchair. It is because I have CP, which stands for Cerebral Palsy. It came from me not getting enough oxygen when I was born. CP can cause problems walking, using your hands, or for some people seeing, hearing, learning, or talking. With me, I can't walk at all or do small things with my fingers on my left hand. So I probably will never be a knitter, but I can do things with my hands like control the joy stick on my chair and hit a tether ball and type pretty fast with one hand.

And even though I cannot walk, I am glad that I can talk. You can't choose your type of CP but my parents remind me that I can choose how I deal with it. Just like a boy that I met who is the opposite of me with his CP. When my mom and I went for a checkup with my CP doctor, I met Ricky. He can use both hands but he can't talk clearly. We were in the waiting room with a bunch of other people a really long time, like two hours. I couldn't understand his speech but he had a big screen attached to his wheelchair that would talk for him in a boy's voice. It sounded natural, not like a robot. For instance, he could push the icon with his picture on it and the computer boy's voice said, "Hi. My name is Ricky" or he could touch the icon of a cup and the voice would say, "Please get me a drink." He could have it say whatever he wanted if he took his time.

So we were talking back and forth and he had it on low volume. Then when his dad left to get coffee, Ricky turned the volume button up to ten and he pushed some buttons. Suddenly a computer woman's voice yelled "Oh darling, kiss my lips! Oh darling, kiss my lips!" Over and over! First people laughed, then they frowned. Then the nurse came out from behind the glass window and asked him to stop, so he did.

Tuesday, July 17th.

OK, enough with the history of me, Aria and Benjamin. Now we are older (our parents are always saying "You kids are growing up so fast" – you would think that parents could come up with something more original to say), and I am thinking that we may not be good friends forever. Because at the end of the school year I realized that my friends don't always see me. It has nothing to do with their eyesight (Aria does wear glasses, but it's not as if her vision is so bad that she can't see me when I am sitting right there). It is all about my Cloak of Invisibility.

I once read a book about a boy who wanted to have a Cloak of Invisibility. He had lots of ideas about what he could do and where he could go if no one could see him. At the time I thought this was a pretty spiffy idea, but that was before I got my own Cloak of Invisibility. Now that I have one, I don't want it at all. I didn't ask for it, and I don't know how to give it back.

The first time I was wearing my Cloak of Invisibility, I didn't even know I had one, or that I had it on. I was sitting in the school lunchroom with lots of kids at the table, and Hannah started talking to Aria about how excited she was that she was going to Aria's upcoming birthday party. Girls only, so Benjamin was not going to be invited. He didn't seem to mind this too much, especially when he heard that Aria's theme was "Spa Day" and all the girls were coming to her house for manicures and pedicures. In fact, wild horses probably could not have dragged Benjamin to the party even if he was invited. Aria's family had moved from our apartment building just the month before, and their home was new and spacious. So Aria started acting beyond excited telling us about her new house and that there was enough room to have a huge birthday party for the first time ever.

But I thought she had kind of a funny look on her face and I didn't know why. There were twelve girls on her guest list, and it looked like just about every girl was going. Then as I was sitting there, picking through mystery meat just like everyone else, I realized that Aria was not looking at me at all when she talked about all the fun things planned for the party. And then I realized that I hadn't received my invitation and the party was the next weekend!

I thought maybe she didn't email invitations; maybe she was just telling her friends in person about the party and asking them to come and she probably didn't think she even needed to ask me, because I had been at every birthday party for her forever, every one of them right there in our apartment building. Or maybe my Mom overlooked the email or figured I already knew about the party. So I asked Aria if any invitations had been emailed and what time the party started so my parents could bring me over. At that moment I realized that Aria and all of the other girls, and even Benjamin, were looking away from me. It was as if I wasn't even there at the lunch table with them. It was like I was invisible! I felt so bad and now I didn't want to look at anyone. I was glad when somebody changed the subject and started in about the geography test that was coming up and how mean Mr. Kelly is to always give so many tests.

Thursday, July 19th.

I am not a whiner. That is not in my vocabulary at all, and I am Gemini-strong. So I don't think it was whining when I told my Mom about the party when I got home after school that day. For a brief moment I thought that I had mysteriously been draped with the Cloak of Invisibility again, because I saw Mom looking away from me. It was just for just a teensy-tiny second, but still. Then my Mom did look at me and she explained that she knew about Aria's party already, but that it wasn't possible or practical for me to go. I was so confused by what my Mom had just said that I couldn't even come up with any of my usual amazing words to respond – the best I could manage was a stunned "huh?"

It was then that my Mom explained that the problem was not me, but my wheelchair. And to be fair, it really isn't the wheelchair that is the problem. The problem is Aria's new house. Her beautiful home has stairs leading up to the front door and steps in the garage to go into the kitchen. It has bathrooms upstairs for Aria's family, and a guest bathroom downstairs for their friends who visit. But that bathroom (or so I hear) has a skinny door that I can't get through. So even if people could help me get into the house (they would have to be strong to carry me up the garage steps, and it can be pretty scary to be carried in a wheelchair) I wouldn't be able to go to the bathroom the entire time that I was there. And I know all the words, good and bad, for what you do in a bathroom. But no matter what you call it, going to the bathroom is a necessity.

I told my Mom that I was confused about all of this. After all, I can go just about anywhere in my wheelchair because of that ADA law stuff. I asked her why it is that I can manage in our apartment just fine, but I can't do that in Aria's super fancy, brand new, big-enough-to-have-a-huge-birthday-party house that I can't go to. Because my Mom is a PWKWD (a Parent with a Kid with a Disability) she has learned a lot because of me (my Dad has, too). You should hear my Mom talk about physical therapy – she knows every part of the body and how it works and sometimes it gets boring when she explains stuff like that to people, but I am not going to say anything to her about that!

So my Mom was able to explain to me that just like there is a law – the ADA – for public places like restaurants and movie theaters and the Children's Museum, there is a law for apartments, too. It is called the Fair Housing Act, the idea being that it wasn't fair in the olden days that people who use a wheelchair like me couldn't find apartments to live in. And there is nothing so different about our apartment – none of our neighbors use wheelchairs, but they like living in our building (it is a pretty cool place to live – our swimming pool is a popular place, and I will now be snarky and point out that Aria with her fancy new house doesn't have a pool to swim in now - unless I invite her over to swim with me – so there).

So it was pretty sequential and logical for me to ask my Mom what law it was that makes houses usable for people with wheelchairs and how come Aria's new house broke the law. After all, public places and lots of apartments are pretty manageable, and I think that is a very good thing. But I was gob-smacked when she told me that there are hardly any laws at all that say that houses have to be built so that people like me can manage. Mom said that while we are very happy living in our apartment right now, that if we want to live in a house someday, we won't have lots of choices. We couldn't really move into Aria's subdivision if we wanted to, since none of those houses would make sense for a KWD.

That didn't make me feel so good – in fact I started to cry and told Mom I am so sorry. I told her I know that having a KWD is not what Mom and Dad planned on (even though I know they love me and think that I am a pretty cool kid to have, especially since Dad always tells me that from the time I was a baby he knew I was a keeper). But the most important part of being a KWD is the K-part. I am a Kid! And I don't want to be the one who is responsible for my family not getting a house. Then my Mom was crying and that made me cry harder. And I felt so bad that I yelled at my Mom and said some pretty mean things to her (and used words I am never, ever supposed to use) and so she wasn't just crying, she was yelling too, and she sent me to my room. At that moment I actually wanted my Cloak of Invisibility – I wanted to disappear from the face of this ugly unfair planet but mostly from my Mom.

Friday, July 20th.

I was on restriction in my room for two days. I really got in trouble for the words I used with my Mom. It didn't matter to me because that was when Aria was having her spa party that I couldn't go to anyway. But then that made me cry more, which really did not make any sense. What a crummy weekend, but at least by Monday my eyes weren't puffy anymore, and Mom and Dad were pretty well over it – although I did have to endure a lecture from my Dad about respecting my parents. My Dad does not cut me any slack.

But if I thought the weekend was crummy, lunch time at school on Monday was even worse. All of the girls were talking about the party and showing off their fingernails with colors, sparkles and flowers. I think Benjamin likes two of the girls because he actually pretended to be interested in their nails. But no one even pretended to be interested in me. In fact, no one even pretended that they knew I was there. I was absolutely and totally invisible AGAIN! And I started to cry, which is not how I wanted to be noticed, so now I wanted to be invisible. How crazy is that? I pretended I had to make an important call to my Mom so I could get away from the table. I even went down the hall toward the principal's office so it would look like I really was going to use the phone. (Our school is very strict and we can't use cell phones during school hours or they confiscate them and then our parents have to come to get them back.)

Saturday, July 21st.

If this summer journal (required, which is totally wrong) were a story about a fictional girl, the writer would have her friends all realize that they were being mean and make her feel better, or the fictional girl would find new friends with houses that she could visit with her wheelchair and she wouldn't need her old friends anymore. But this isn't about a fictional girl, this is about me – Libby. And I can't go to my friend Aria's house and that makes me want to cry again because I miss seeing her as often as I used to. I haven't seen her much this summer.

Monday, July 23rd.

Yesterday Aria called me; she said that she and Benjamin were going to the mall and could my parents drop me off to shop and eat in the food court with them. I was going to say no because (1) I don't want to be asked to do things with my friends only when it is convenient for them and (2) I wanted them to think I had better things to do than just hang out with them. But I really wanted to hang out with them! So I said yes.

Mom loaded me in the van and we both went into the mall (my Mom is not one to get within 100 feet of a mall and not actually go shopping). We went to the fountain in the middle of the atrium and there were Aria and Benjamin. Mom gave me the drill (she has this memorized) – meet her back in exactly two hours; keep our cell phones on; stick together; money for lunch; bring her the change.

We browsed around in the video game store and then a clothes shop (Benjamin nagged us to hurry up the whole time). We went to the food court and got our favorite mall food which is the Chinese shrimp fried rice plate with egg rolls. Benjamin pointed with his chin and told us to look a couple of tables over at some guy. Benjamin was impressed because he was "ripped" and I could see what he meant. The guy had major arm muscles and Aria said she liked his cute hair cut (a hair cut has nothing to do with being ripped, however). He was wearing a tee-shirt that said "Murderball" with a picture of a wheelchair and flames coming from the back wheels. I wondered what "Murderball" meant and why there was a picture of a wheelchair on his shirt. I told Benjamin to go ask him (because Benjamin is a guy) and he told me I should go ask (because I have a wheelchair). Then Aria got up, made some comment about wimps, and went over to the guy herself.

Because my teachers will be reading this journal (because it is an unfair summer assignment for school) they will probably get all worked up that Aria went over to talk to some guy. But there were lots of people all around us and Benjamin and I were watching her and the guy very closely. I admit I was kind of impressed that she would do this (it was probably the hair cut that convinced her). So there they are talking, and Aria is pointing at us and the guy is looking at us, and we're looking back at him, and then the guy pushed back from the table and rolled right over to us in his wheelchair! Not only did the wheelchair surprise me (it was one of those low ones, like a racing chair, that I could not see because of the table), I have never actually talked with a grownup in a wheelchair (except for that old lady in the movie bathroom, and she mostly lectured me so that wasn't really a conversation). So I was both excited and nervous because the empty seat at our table was next to me and this guy just smoothly pulled up and introduced himself to Benjamin and me.

It turns out that Everett (which I think is a very nice name) is a Murderball athlete. Murderball is one name for rugby played in wheelchairs (but it is a special kind of rugby that is part basketball, part ice hockey and part handball, too). You have to be disabled to play and at least three of your limbs have to be affected. I admit when Everett told us that that I sneaked a peek at his hands and noticed that one of his hands is missing two fingers and looks kind of crooked. (I wonder if looking was rude, because I really was interested. Maybe some of the people who I sometimes think are rude for looking at me are interested in my disability, but in a good way.)

People play Murderball in lots of countries (Everett said dozens) and they use specially designed manual wheelchairs. He said that there was even a movie made about Murderball and it was nominated for an Oscar. We thought maybe Everett was a movie star (that cute hair cut!) but he laughed and said no, although he and his wife did go to see the movie. They didn't take their little kids because there was too much cursing, but maybe Mom will rent it for me because I am older (although she might say no because of the movie cursing – she still hasn't forgotten what I said when I had that meltdown about Aria's party). But I will tell her I want to see a movie where the people with disabilities aren't all nice and sweet and happy and stuff – sometimes I want to gag. And I don't like movies about crabby disabled people who get saved by super-great able-bodied people (I saw movie like that once).

Everett told us that he has fallen out of his chair when playing and one time he cracked his head on the gym floor, but not all teams play that rough. He looked right at me and told me that there are girls teams in some cities, which is exactly what I was wondering. Everett was really paying attention to me, and I think that for a moment Aria and Benjamin got a taste of what it is like to be invisible (and I may not be nice for thinking that, but it made me happy for just a minute). I mean he was paying attention to me as me, not that kind of weird attention that people give me sometimes, where they say "Don't speed, you might get a ticket". Or they smile with their lips tight and the smile doesn't last long.

So, I was sort of basking in this attention when Benjamin all of a sudden said "Did you know Libby still can't get into people's houses? She can't get through their bathroom doors either." I don't know where that came from. I didn't think that Benjamin had really realized about houses, and for a second I was embarrassed and a little bit mad at him for bringing this up. But then I loved him for doing it (not love-love! the friend-kind-of-love). It was like both Everett and Benjamin had read my mind in the past fifteen minutes.

I decided I should start speaking up and I told Everett I get pretty disappointed. My Mom says I sometimes have to be realistic and accept that is the way the world is. Everett looked surprised at that and said he wanted to maybe talk to my Mom about houses. I told him she would be meeting up with us soon, but he said he had to leave now to go pick up his own kids from their karate class. Then he wrote his phone number on a napkin for me and said he would really like it if Mom would call him.

Tuesday, July 24th.

Yesterday, when it was time to meet back up with my Mom at the mall, we went back to the fountain. When we saw her, we all started talking at once about Everett. She was a bit concerned at first about "some guy" we had spent time with, but when she realized we had used good judgment and not gone off alone with him, she was really interested to hear about Murderball and that Everett had kids and cute hair. I showed her the napkin with the phone number and she copied it into her cell phone. I kept the napkin just because it felt like a good souvenir and when I got home I sealed it in a sandwich bag and put it in my miscellaneous drawer, which is also my sock drawer. I may not walk, but I take my feet seriously – I have lots of cute socks and a pretty good selection of shoes.

Wednesday, July 25th.

I'm really excited! Mom said she talked to Dad and called Everett and we are all invited to Everett's house on Saturday for a cookout with his wife and kids, and Aria and Ben are invited, too!

Sunday, July 29th.

Yesterday Benjamin came over to our apartment and we all loaded up in the van. Then we went by Aria's house to pick her up and I admit I did not want to look at it. I only saw it out of the corner of my eye – it is stone and has red shutters.

Everett was on his front porch when we got to his house and he came out to the driveway to meet us. He shook hands with Mom and Dad. I noticed he was using his crooked hand and not even thinking about it. He led us through the garage to the back yard where the grill was going and there was a lot of food on the picnic table. Then his wife Tovah came out in the yard with the kids. They are twin boys three years old, but not identical, Austin and Anthony. Austin was kind of shy and he held on to the bottom of Tovah's skirt. But Anthony ran right over to me and climbed right up on my front pedals looking at me with a big grin. He must have seen a bunch of people in wheelchairs with his dad and the Murderball team. He asked me if he could have a ride. Actually he said a "wide" and it was really cute. I looked over at Everett and he nodded yes and Dad said "Go really slow" (which I was already going to do. It's annoying when grown ups tell me to do something that makes perfect sense.) So I started driving around and Anthony was holding onto my legs and laughing. I totally did not feel like I had on a Cloak of Invisibility.

Then we ate the burgers and other things Everett and Tovah had made. (My mom just told me how to spell Tovah which is a Hebrew name, and the 'h' is silent.) Then Mom took out the cake from the box. She had offered to bring dessert. It was a carrot cake with cream cheese frosting from Maroni's, which is a very good bakery. Tovah invited us to have dessert inside because even though the sun was starting to go down it was still pretty hot outside.

Tovah went away for a while to give the twins a bath and put them to bed and Everett made coffee. Dad offered to help him carry in the coffee from the kitchen (and fizzy water for Aria, Benjamin and me) and helped pass around the plates with cake.

After a while Everett said he remembered in the mall we had started talking about houses and how they don't have access. He said he really understood why I said I feel disappointed sometimes. That is how I knew he remembered exactly what I said! He said he and Tovah have to turn down some invitations because there always seem to be steps, and they think they don't even get some invitations to turn down, and they really feel like it cuts down their social life.

He said it is sad that houses are still built so that people who can't walk can't get into them. All the other new buildings for the public and apartments have changed, but houses are still built like back in the dark ages. Then he said that some people around the country are trying to change that and get every new house to be built so they can be visited by people like us. I thought "Wow!" Everett said it isn't even hard to make new houses better for people with disabilities – they just need one way to get in without steps and wide enough doors to get in the bathroom, which are the most important things. Everett said not to be rude, but he had read in some disability magazine where somebody called it "Get in and pee."

Everett said the people trying to change how houses are built are calling it "visitability". I thought he was saying visibility, like something is easy to see, and I thought about my cloak. My Dad misunderstood too, so he asked, "Visibility"?

Everett said actually no, visit-ability, the ability to visit, and there were actually towns that had laws that every new house had to be built that way. "Really?" said Dad, and he sounded kind of doubtful.

Everett said yes and he said the names of the towns and that tens of thousands of visitable houses had already been built in those towns.

I was feeling super-excited. If houses were built that way, kids wouldn't have to feel bad that they couldn't be in people's houses and miss birthday parties and sleepovers. And able-bodied kids wouldn't have to feel bad that their friends could not visit them even if they were best friends, and had all their little funny shared jokes and plans they made together, and had been together all their lives like me and my friends.

Aria asked if we could make a law like that in Waunegua. (That is the name of our town, which I know my teacher Mrs. Brock who assigned this journal already knows, but I am giving that information in case someone reads this in the future who is not from Waunegua and wonders where I live.) "It's possible we could make a law like that. But that kind of change usually takes a lot of time and work," Everett said. "For instance: Do you ever see people with disabilities getting on the bus, or waiting at the bus stop?" "Sure," said Aria." I saw it just the other day. A ramp folded out of the bus and the guy wheeled on."

Everett said getting public buses to be accessible had taken a long time. An older guy on his Murderball team, George, had told him he was one of the people who helped make a law for a wheelchair lift to be on every new bus. He had gone to jail a few times for blocking inaccessible buses.

"Jail?!" Aria asked, "What did they do?" Everett said they chained themselves to buses that didn't have lifts so the buses couldn't drive away. They often stayed for hours, until the police came and arrested them. I asked why they didn't just try to make a law in the first place. Everett said they did try, over and over, but no one was taking them really seriously. They decided they had to bump up the action, get some publicity, turn up the heat. Everett said that as a matter of fact, he has a picture of George from an old newspaper and Everett wheeled over to a drawer and pulled out a folder and found the photo. He brought it over to us. I looked at it for quite a while. I was amazed.

©Photo by Tom Olin

"Whoa!" said Benjamin. "Which one is George?" Everett said it was the guy on the far right side wearing the shades and head band. He had the wheel of his chair chained to the bus wheel. George and hundreds of others did this year after year, at the same time working for laws to get passed, and eventually "A lift on every new bus" became the law of the land. PWDs and their families and friends all over the country celebrated with victory parties.

Everett asked if we wanted a copy of the picture and we all did, so he went into another room and came back in a minute and gave us the copies.

"Maybe I could take action for houses," I said, sort of quietly. I wasn't feeling like I would know what to do Ben and Aria said they wanted to help, and that made me feel more confident. My Dad said, "Yes, I think you kids could make a difference." He said maybe we could give some speeches to our class. Or write a letter to the newspaper. "Absolutely," Everett said. "Even small actions get people thinking. People can start seeing new things that before just seemed the way things would always be.'"

Then it was time to go and Mom thanked Everett and Tovah and said she would like to invite their family to our place. It sounded like she meant it instead of those things adults say sometimes and later you figure out they didn't really mean it. I really hope they will come over.

Monday, July 30th.

Aria, Benjamin and I can't think of what to do for our action about houses. We want to do something better than just giving a boring speech to class or writing a boring letter to the newspaper. We have already had two meetings and don't have any good ideas. I think maybe we might have to wait until we are adults.

Tuesday, July 31st.

I can't believe it! We have a big empty lot right near our apartment building and today there was a huge banner on the chain link fence that says "Coming Your Way: 24 Luxury Homes." They had smoothed over the ground and pipes were sticking up showing where the houses would be. When Benjamin and I saw this we had the same idea. Let's make these houses be visitable! They aren't even built yet! We called up Aria and told her and she is excited, too. When I told my Mom, she was enthralled. Well, maybe she wasn't extremely enthralled, but she listened closely and suggested that maybe we should ask the builder to build all 24 new houses visitable. The name Wilkes Quality Homes and a phone number are on the banner.

Wednesday, August 15th.

I am going to have to write and write here because I got way behind on this journal and that is not a good thing with school starting in 3 weeks. But we were really busy with our plan. Mom helped me and Benjamin and Aria write a letter to the head of Wilkes Quality Homes, Mr. Phillip Wilkes. She got his email address off the website and let us use her email account to send the letter.

Then she said we should do our "follow up call". We chose Benjamin to make the call because I had already spent a lot of time typing the email from what we had written and Aria had a summer cold and her voice sounded funny. Mom helped Benjamin practice what to say. Then after all that practice, all he got was voice mail, so he got super nervous and didn't say anything and hung up. Then Mom helped him practice what he should say to leave a message, saying that we wanted the new houses to be visitable and asking for an appointment to discuss it further. Then when Benjamin called again that time he got a real live person instead of voicemail, and he was so nervous he said "Sorry, wrong number" and hung up again.

Aria and I were laughing our heads off. Benjamin got kind of mad for a few minutes and then asked Mom if she would make the call. She did it all smooth and nice and remembered everything like asking for an appointment.

These things are easier for grown ups because they have had lots of practice. The person on the phone said she had gotten our email, and she gave us an appointment for 3:00 the next afternoon. Mom had to take us in the van because it was on the other side of town. We got there a little bit early because Mom said that was the right thing to do. I waited for Mom to speak to the receptionist but Mom nodded at me. "Hello, we have an appointment with Mr. Wilkes," I squeaked. My voice came out funny. The receptionist looked at her computer screen. She said, "Oh yes! Mr. Wilkes was called away last minute to a meeting, but he asked his assistant Miss Henning to speak with you." The receptionist made a call and a young woman with short red hair came in, smiling. "I'm so glad you could come!"

We all went into the conference room (I had never been in one before – there was a really big table and lots of chairs with cushions and small wheels on their legs, and large framed pictures of houses that I guess had all been built by Mr. Wilkes) and Aria explained our purpose, and Ben showed photos of accessible houses he had downloaded from a Visitability website. I ended our presentation with the line I had practiced, "And that is why we would like your company to build all your new houses with one entrance that does not have any steps and bathrooms that have wide enough doors!"

"Those are really nice houses in the photos," Miss Henning said. "But I'm not sure they are quite practical for us. You see, none of our buyers so far are wheelchair bound." (Ugh – I hate when people say "wheelchair bound". I am not tied with a rope to my chair.) "But wait!" Aria said to her. "They might get disabled later! Or they might make friends with someone in a wheelchair! Or maybe they are fighting for America in a war and they are a wounded warrior when they come home and need to find a house to live in." Miss Henning smiled. "That's a very good point!" she said. Mom said nothing. "Will you keep this folder of pictures and pass it on to Mr. Wilkes?" Ben asked, holding out the folder. "I certainly will," said Miss Henning. "I am sure he will give this very serious consideration. And he'll call you if he needs further information."

Mom took us all for milkshakes at The Speckled Cow and we were very excited about the meeting. "You kids handled yourselves very well," she said. Aria said, "Miss Henning said he will give this serious consideration! And I think Mr. Wilkes will decide to do the access because he'll realize what a good idea it is". "He very well might!" Mom said with a big smile, but her eyebrows were raised up in a way that made me wonder if she really believed that.

Benjamin and I watched the building lot every day and we reported to Aria. The houses started going up really fast. But it sure looked like the first houses had a step on the front. "Maybe the zero step entrances are around the back," Benjamin said. "Remember how we told them a back entrance was okay too if someone could get to it in a wheelchair? Let's check the backs tomorrow before the workers get there."

The next morning we went out really early and down the street to the building lot. Benjamin looked around. No workers in sight. I waited on the sidewalk while Benjamin went on reconnaissance, a word I learned last year in social studies. He came back looking shocked. "Steps, steps, steps!" he said. "Up the front, and up the back and from the garages into the house!"

My face sort of felt like concrete was pulling down my cheeks. "Mr. Wilkes didn't even ask us for more information," I said.

We reported to Aria. We decided to have a meeting at noon on the playground. The three of us went behind a tree near the fence and instead of playing dodge ball or tetherball like we usually did, we made another plan.

The next morning Benjamin came by our apartment. "Can Libby come with me to the park to meet Aria and have a picnic? My mom made some sandwiches." Mom said OK as long as I kept my cell phone on and promised to be back by two. She put some peaches and bananas into a plastic bag for us.

We met Aria as planned at the statue of the guy on a horse and Benjamin stuffed our food under a bush. We sat on a bench (well, they sat on the bench) and counted the money we had all taken out of our banks. $56 dollars and 20 cents. Not bad, that would do it from the prices I had found on line.

"We have to move fast to get done by two," I said. We headed up the block, crossing three streets. We got to the hardware store, and took out our list and money. Twenty feet of chain, $26.45. Two padlocks $9.29 each. Plus tax. We decided to use the change to buy some Twizzlers which were sitting by the checkout. We had just enough money left so that Aria could go into the craft store and buy a roll of drawing paper.

At the park we barely had enough time to practice wrapping and twining ourselves together with the chain and pretending to lock it, and then scarf our sandwiches and fruit, so I could make it back home by 2:00. Aria took the stuff we bought to her house to hide in her big new garage.

"Did you have a good time?" Mom asked Benjamin and me when we got home. I told her yes and I gave her details about a skateboarder and an almost dog fight we had seen, and what kind of sandwiches we had, but not all the details obviously. We asked my Mom if she would make sandwiches because we wanted to have another picnic day tomorrow. She said yes, same rules as today.

Benjamin and I had figured out the workers were never at the building lot until 8:00 a.m. because we could hear the bulldozer faintly from our apartment building. Without permission (our picnic lunch was for later in the morning) Benjamin and I went to the building lot and Aria was already there. There was the lot, no workers yet, with a few new houses and the bulldozer and stacks of wood and bricks. A couple of other kids and a mother were walking past but they did not pay any attention to us. My heart started pounding. "Now!" I said, and we all took off. I had my chair on high speed and Benjamin and Aria were running. The ground was really bumpy. I was afraid for a minute I would tip.

I pulled up super-close to the bulldozer. Benjamin swung the chain around one of the bars that leads to the scoop thing, then around one of my wheels, around my waist, then around my other wheel. Then Ben and Aria wound it tight around their waists. Then Aria got the locks out of her pack and they locked the chain tight in two places.

Then we put the keys where we had planned. Inside the waist band of my underpants. I had worn jeans instead of a dress just for that purpose. We thought it would be illegal for anyone to look in my underpants.

Aria was shaking. We tried to calm down. Some people on the sidewalk were already looking at us. Aria pulled out the two long signs she had made with markers from the roll of drawing paper. I held up "Access To Houses Is Needed". Our other one was better, it said "Houses Un-visitable Make Us Irritable!" Aria held that up.

A little while later some workers in hard hats came onto the lot and looked at us from a distance. One made a call on his phone. Benjamin, Aria and I were saying things to encourage each other. We were suddenly scared.

In a couple of minutes, another man pulled up in a pick-up truck, got out and walked over to us. He seemed like a boss kind of person. He asked us what we were doing. We told him we were doing "civil disobedience" to get the houses to have access. "That may be what you want, but I'm afraid that is not your decision," he said. Something about the way he said that made me feel very annoyed, even if I was still scared.

"What you are doing is against the law. Every minute that we can't use this machine is costing us money. I need you to unlock these locks and go home" he said pretty loudly. We were quiet and more scared than ever. He put out his hand. "If you won't unlock the locks, give me the keys and I will do it. Now!" he said.

"Ummmm....the keys are not available at this time," said Aria.

The not-very-smart-thing was, this was the end of our plan - we had not really thought about what we would do next (so much for planning). So, we sat there. He stood there. He walked away and made a phone call.

Then we heard a siren, and a police car screeched up. Two policemen got out. One of them was carrying a big hedge-clipper kind of thing and started walking over to us. I started thinking, why did we do this? Benjamin and Aria looked really scared.

Next a van pulled up with "Wanegua Weekly Chronicle" on the side. A man with a camera and a woman with a notebook and a microphone got out.

The reporter woman came up to us, and the boss too. Then the police. One of the policemen said in a nice voice, "Children, we need you to unlock yourselves immediately and leave the premises. This is private property. "

"We can't," said Benjamin. "We have to do civil disobedience." I saw the cameraman laugh. He started to take pictures of what was going on. "Believe me, you have already done civil disobedience," the policeman said, and this time his voice wasn't so nice. "I need you to give me the keys to the locks or I'm going to have to cut the chains. And I don't want you to get hurt."

We didn't say anything. I was too embarrassed to reach into the top of my pants, where I could feel that they keys had slipped down a little, especially with the camera pointed at me. Plus I thought that George would not have given them the keys when he was chained to the bus. So we just sat there.

The policeman finally took the clipper and cut the chain, which pulled on the chain and squeezed us a little but not too bad. Meanwhile the cameraman was clicking away. The reporter lady was talking to us, asking us why we were there, and our names and where we lived, and writing in her notebook. Then the talking policeman said he was walking Benjamin and me home to our parents, and told the other policeman to take Aria in the police car to her house.

Thursday, August 16th.

I was immediately grounded for life by my parents. Benjamin and Aria and I were restricted from talking on the phone, so I don't know what their parents did to them.

Friday, August 17th.

My parents must have thought more about me being on restriction because they called me into the living room for a talk. They both sat down so I knew it was a big deal. They told me they understood that houses need to be built with access and they understood that we chained ourselves to the bulldozer to make people notice and change their behavior. But I had to promise not to do anything illegal again.

I said in my opinion people had to do civil disobedience until changes happen. They said that is for adults and asked me to promise not to do it again until I was 21 years old. I said how about 18 years old, that is when Ben's step- brother went into the Army. I saw my dad try not to smile. They said okay. They wrote on a piece of paper "I Libby Benson solemnly promise I will not take part in any illegal actions, under any circumstances, until I am 18 years of age." I signed my name.

My cell phone rang and it was Ben. He said he had to promise not to break the law and Aria did too. We figured the parents must have talked to each other.

Saturday, August 18th.

The Wanegua newspaper came out and we are on the front page! With a picture of us! The headline says "Area Kids Protest at Housing Site". The picture shows us crossing the field with the two policemen. Aria is quoted saying why we wanted all the houses to have access, and Benjamin is quoted saying we brought information to Mr. Wilkes but he didn't do the access. It quoted me saying people all around the country are trying to make houses have Visitability. But it ended with a quote from Mr. Wilkes. The reporter must have called him up because he was not there when we did our civil disobedience. His quote said, "What great spirit these kids were showing. Unfortunately of course it is not practical to put features for the disabled in every house. But we are glad to work with any buyer who has unusual challenges."

I was kind of upset that he got to say the last word. And I was very upset that he said "unusual". What is "unusual" about wanting to visit your friends? What is "unusual" even if you do not have a disability like me, about wanting to keep living in your own house when you get old and have arthritis, or if you get hurt in an accident? Everyone wants that. But I was glad we were in the paper.

Mom got a bunch of calls all afternoon from her friends who saw the article. I got calls from Hannah and Luke who are in my class. Luke said congratulations and it was cool we were with the police. Hannah said her mother thought it was terrible we were doing a crime. I tried to explain how doing a crime to make things better was not the same as doing a crime like robbery, but Hannah said it was the same. I don't think I explained it very well.

Monday, August 20th.

Today my Mom got a phone call and email from Mr. Wilkes. He asked if we could come to his office tomorrow morning at 10:00, Aria and Benjamin too. He said he has a surprise for us. Mom said yes. He told her what the surprise is but she promised not to tell us.

Tuesday, August 21st.

The best surprise ever! Better than $1,000. When we got to the office two older men came up to us. We had never seen Mr. Wilkes before so we didn't know which one he was until he introduced us to the other man. Mr. Callahan was tall, partly grey haired and mostly bald. Mr. Wilkes was also bald. He had a fringe of black hair all around the bald spot, even the front. That looked kind of weird but I did not stare.

Mr. Wilkes said, "Kids, I have some good news for you. We are going to build all the rest of our new houses with a zero-step entrance and wide enough doors, including the bathroom doors. We have four houses already built that are un-Visitable, as you saw, but the other 20 will all be built Visit-able."

I smiled so big my cheeks almost hurt. Benjamin and Aria said "thank you!" at the same time. My mom was looking half like she was going to cry with happiness.

"Here's what made up my mind," said Mr. Wilkes. "I have to admit I was embarrassed to have you kids on the front page of the paper saying I was doing something wrong. But I also thought maybe there was some slight chance you were right. Then I got a call from my old friend here, Mr. Callahan."

Mr. Callahan is a retired home builder and he and Mr. Wilkes used to be together in the same home builders club. He said last year his wife tripped on a cart at the grocery store and broke one leg and one wrist. Then when she came home from the hospital she could hardly get around in her own house. Mr. Callahan had to get the neighbors to help carry her in and out of the house in her wheelchair, even if she just wanted to get out in their rose garden to sit in the fresh air. And she could not even fit her wheelchair through the bathroom door. So she had to go to the bathroom in a special adult-sized potty in their hall. This went on for a whole month until she was healed enough to walk on crutches.

After that, Mr. Callahan made a promise to himself that he would help people who had something like that happen, so that they could manage in their house no matter how long they might be disabled. And he also wanted our soldiers who come home with disabilities to be able to live with their families or find their own houses to live in. So when he saw us on the front page of the paper, he knew this was his chance. He studied information about Visitability on the Internet. Then he called his friend Mr. Wilkes and told him that he wanted to show him how he could make entrances with no steps that look great and do not cost much. He helped Mr. Wilkes draw the doors wider on the house diagrams and showed how to move the dirt so the sidewalks would come up to the porches without a step.

Mr. Wilkes said, "Kids, we want to have a big celebration when we finish the first Visitable house. We want you to come and officially cut the ribbon. Will you do that?"

We said yes, and I was thinking, "A thousand times yes!"

Saturday, November 17th.

And that ladies and gentlemen was the end of my summer journal. I turned it in when school started and am proud to say that I made an A+ on that project. (Although I hope I never have that big a summer assignment ever again.) I think my teachers and the principal were impressed with what Ben, Aria and I accomplished, which probably helped my grade. I decided I should add more to the journal because people who might read this some day might want to know what happened next.

Today was the grand opening of the first visitable house! It seemed like about a hundred people squeezed together in the front yard. Mr. Wilkes asked Aria, Benjamin and me to come up on the porch. It felt so great to go up there with my friends without any special ramp, just the sidewalk. Mr. Wilkes' assistant tied a red ribbon with a big bow across the posts. Mr. Wilkes gave me a big scissors and told me it was time to cut the ribbon. The photographer from the paper took pictures.

I looked out at all the people in the yard. Mom and Dad, Ben and Aria's parents and brothers and sisters, Everett, Tovah, the twins, and a lot of people I didn't know. I felt happier than I've ever felt.

Then suddenly in my imagination it was night, not day, with a bright moon. I was flying high above the ground in my wheelchair, above the trees, with my Cape of Visitability unfurled behind me. Below me were dark hills, a shining river, and houses with their lights on. With a silver sword I was slashing side to side, slashing out all unfairness in the world. From the houses other kids started flying up one by one, sort of in spirals Some were on horses, some in wheelchairs, some on bicycles, some just flying with their arms, and all of us were sailing together across the earth.

In a second I was back to day again and it was time to go into the house for a reception, which means everyone talked to everyone else and we all ate cookies and cupcakes and drank punch. I could drink the punch without worrying about going to the bathroom later because I knew I could fit through the door with my wheelchair. After while Mr. Wilkes came over to Arla, Benjamin and me. He said he learned something important from us and thanked us.

Friday, November 23rd.

The newspaper came today. There was a picture on the front page like last time but this time it was of us cutting the ribbon, with Mr. Wilkes behind us. He said good things about Visitability in the article. He said a lot of people were buying the houses and hardly anyone even noticed that there was no step up to the porch. One woman actually said she was glad her father could visit her now, because in her old house he could not come up the steps with his cane. And we heard that a wounded warrior was going to be buying one of the other visitable houses that Mr. Wilkes had built. My mom scanned the article into the computer and also pasted it into her scrapbook, she said "for posterity". I looked up posterity in the dictionary.

Yesterday it was Thanksgiving and we went to see my grandparents.

While we were driving I saw a lot of houses that were un-visitable and it made me feel sad, and it also made me angry, too, because making houses visitable is not that hard to do. But Everett said we planted a seed (idea) and got a lot of publicity and Visitability will grow.

At night when I'm falling asleep, sometimes I feel like I'm flying again, wearing my cape, and all the kids are flying with their swords, slashing out more unfairness. I think

I will still remember that when I am old. I hope then all houses will be built so that everybody with and without disabilities can visit each other. I think that maybe I can even work to make that happen. Maybe other kids and grownups will, too. Because as Everett says,

"Even Small Actions Get People Thinking"

Libby and the Cape of Visitability Reader's Guide

This is a visitable house like the one where Libby, Benjamin and Aria cut the ribbon. Does this look like a regular house to you?

Here a boy is arriving for a party at a visitable house. He is happy to be able to come to the party and doesn't his friend look excited too.

Here are some of the pictures Benjamin gave Mr. Wilkes at the meeting.

Can you see that it is rather easy to make houses visitable?

Bolingbrook, Illinois — Every new house with access since 2002.

Pima County, Arizona --- Every new house with access since 2002.

Accessible entrance at the back of a house on a steep lot.

Accessible Entrance from the Garage.

Discussion questions for KWDs (with any kind of disability, not just wheel-chair-users):

Are there things you wish non-disabled people would not do or say, related to your disability?

Are there things you are glad non-disabled people do or say, related to your disability?

What is something you do better than other people because you have your disability?

Discussion questions for kids who do not have any disabilities:

Do you know anyone with a disability, young or old? What kind of disability? Do you know what problems they might be facing?

Are there any thoughts or feelings or worries you have that might make you uncomfortable when you are around a PWD?

What makes it easy, or would make it easier, for you to be around a PWD?

Discussion questions for all kids:

Does Libby really have a Cloak of Invisibility and a Cape of Visitability? Can you explain what she is really trying to say when she talks about her cloak and cape?

Can you think of an invention that has been made to help a PWD? (This could be for people who have trouble reading, hearing, seeing, talking, walking, remembering, or any other kind of disability).

Can you think of a new invention no one has made yet that could help a PWD?

If you know people who can't walk or who have troubles walking, can they come to your house?

Everett says "Even small actions get people thinking." Do you agree? Have you or anyone in your family ever worked to solve a big problem by starting out with small actions? Explain what was done.

Do you think it is a good idea to build houses so that people like Libby can visit them?

What else can Libby and her friends do so that more visitable houses are built? What could you do?

Resources for Learning More About Visitability

www.concretechange.org

www.udeworld.com/visitability.html

Darren Larsen's Visitability message
www.youtube.com/watch?v=b9quoouoaea

Building Better Neighborhoods, Part 1
www.youtube.com/watch?v=kuymto17xuo

Building Better Neighborhoods, Part 2
www.youtube.com/watch?v=js9iasjxuts

Increasing Home Access: Designing for Visitability
(for this AARP policy paper, search the above title on line)

www.nationalfairhousing.org

www.adapt.org

About Nadeen Green

Nadeen has been an attorney for many years and through her work as Senior Counsel with For Rent Media Solutions™ and Homes.com she has been able to teach and write about fair housing laws, including those requiring that newer apartment communities have basic design features that provide accessibility. (Nadeen blogs at fairhousing.forrent.com as Fair Housing Lady). But Nadeen really did not fully understand the problems for PWDs when it comes to houses until her work brought her and Eleanor together. The two women have become good friends, each bringing their talents and experiences (Nadeen has written other books for children) to the story of Libby. She hopes this story can be one of those "small actions that will get people thinking".

About Eleanor Smith

Eleanor Smith got polio at age three, before there was
a vaccine to protect people from getting that virus. In
her wheelchair, she attended public school and later
earned a Master's Degree. Over the years she taught in a
high school in Kansas, in an elementary school in Puerto
Rico, and in colleges in Indiana and Georgia. At about
age 40, she was delighted to discover the hard-working,
exuberant disability rights movement. Along with several
hundred other allies in the movement, she did civil
disobedience by blocking buses and did other actions that
caused "a lift on every new bus" to become a requirement
of the ADA. Participating in that quest led to her new
idea: "A zero-step entrance on every new house!" With
that as a goal, she founded Concrete Change in 1987.
People from all around the country have joined this work
for Visitability. At age 70 she retired from Concrete
Change, knowing that the work will continue until access
to homes becomes the normal way to build. Someday

people will think "I can't believe we ever built houses where PWDs couldn't visit or live!" Since 1999, she has lived in a 100% visitable, inter-generational community in Atlanta, where kids often hop a ride on her wheelchair.

Eleanor Smith and Nadeen Green want to thank the following children for being pre-publication reviewers for our book...

Luisa Dutchersmith
Zidia Gibson
Jessica Hall
Adam Huschle
Connor Li
Kelsey Li
Kaeden Lipp
Christina McNamara
Ella Kaufmann Smith
Ty Taliaferro
Austin Thomas
Ruy Tobar
Matthew Vincent
Eleanor (Ella) Wuichet
Jacob Yoder-Schrock

...and the entire 3rd grade class of Mrs. Gidget Smith, Newton County Theme School, Covington, GA.

A special thanks to Mr. Tom Olin for being generous in allowing us to use his historic photo of civil disobedience on behalf of "a lift on every bus".

A special thanks also goes out to Lester de la Cruz for his technical design abilities and to Rodrigo Tobar in his creative artistic abilities ,which have allowed Eleanor and Nadeen's book to come to life.

Nadeen wants to acknowledge the support and help provided by For Rent Media Solutions. This is an example of why she has been proud to work for this company for so many years.

CPSIA information can be obtained
at www.ICGtesting.com
Printed in the USA
LVIC04n1811090414
381021LV00010B/93